Pee Wees on Skis

YEARLING BOOKS/YOUNG YEARLINGS/YEARLING CLASSICS are designed especially to entertain and enlighten young people. Patricia Reilly Giff, consultant to this series, received a bachelor's degree from Marymount College and a master's degree in history from St. John's University. She holds a Professional Diploma in Reading and a Doctorate of Humane Letters from Hofstra University. She was a teacher and reading consultant for many years, and is the author of numerous books for young readers.

Pee Wees on Skis

JUDY DELTON

Illustrated by Alan Tiegreen

A YEARLING BOOK

Published by
Bantam Doubleday Dell Books for Young Readers
a division of
Bantam Doubleday Dell Publishing Group, Inc.
1540 Broadway
New York, New York 10036

ISBN: 0-440-40885-7

Printed in the United States of America

October 1993

21 20 19 18 17 16 15 14 13 12

CWO

With thanks to Winnie Shaffner
and all her young readers

Contents

CHAPTER 1

New Badge Talk

"I'm freezing!" said Tracy Barnes, jumping up and down on the sidewalk.

"I'm not," said Lisa Ronning, letting her coat blow open in the wind. "I'm hot. My new goose-down coat makes me really hot."

Lisa twirled around, showing off her new coat. "My aunt just bought it for me."

"For Christmas?" asked Tracy.

"No," said Lisa. "Just for nothing. I'm her favorite niece."

"It makes you look like a football player." Roger White laughed.

Roger pretended to tackle Lisa, and the other boys joined him. They walked around

with their chests out like football players with lots of padding.

"You're just jealous," said Lisa, "because you haven't got an aunt who buys you down jackets."

"It wasn't cold this morning," said Mary Beth Kelly, her teeth chattering. "Maybe it's going to snow."

"Nah," said Roger. "It won't snow already. It won't snow till winter."

"It is winter, dummy," said Rachel Meyers.

Sonny Stone shook his head. "It's not winter till it snows," he said.

"Winter comes whether it snows or not," said Kevin Moe. "Some winters there isn't any snow at all, and it's still winter."

No one could argue with Kevin, thought Molly Duff. Kevin was the smartest one in second grade. And he was the smartest one in Pee Wee Scout Troop 23.

It was Tuesday, and the Pee Wees were on

the way to their Pee Wee Scout meeting at Mrs. Peters's house. She was their troop leader. There were eleven Scouts all together.

"Look, I can see my breath!" shouted Tim Noon. "That's a sure sign of winter."

Kevin shook his head. "It doesn't have to be winter to see your breath."

"It's not winter till it snows," insisted Sonny again.

"What a baby," said Mary Beth to Molly. "He never listens to anybody. He always thinks he's right."

Sonny was a baby. Molly felt sorry for him. He still had training wheels on his bike, and he was seven. For a long time he hadn't had a father, and his mother babied him. He was an only child.

But Molly was an only child, too, and she wasn't a baby. Anyway, now Sonny's mother was married to the fire chief, and

Sonny had a new adopted brother and sister. But he was still a baby.

By the time the Pee Wees got to Mrs. Peters's house, even Lisa had pulled her coat up over her head to keep warm.

"Come in, come in!" called their leader. "Winter is here!"

"See?" said Kevin.

It was one thing not to believe Kevin, thought Molly. But no one could not believe Mrs. Peters. Scout leaders did not lie.

"What rosy cheeks you all have." Mrs. Peters laughed. "And red noses! Come into the kitchen for some hot cocoa!"

"We never have refreshments till after the meeting," said Molly to Mary Beth. Molly did not like a change in the routine.

"And we never have it in the kitchen," said Mary Beth.

"We need our hot chocolate early today," said Mrs. Peters, "to warm us up!"

The Pee Wees hung up their wraps and gathered around the Peterses' big round kitchen table.

"Marsholows!" shouted Nick, Mrs. Peters's baby.

The Pee Wees laughed.

"He means marshmallows," said Mrs. Stone, who was assistant troop leader. "He loves them."

Sure enough, Nick was stuffing marshmallows into his mouth one after the other. His little cheeks puffed out like two pumpkins.

The Pee Wees began to stuff marshmallows into their mouths.

"Look," called Sonny. "I can get six in my mouth at once."

His mother frowned.

Molly put her marshmallows in her hot chocolate. "I like it when they melt," she said.

"I thought we'd have our meeting here

6

today, instead of in the basement," said their leader. "It's a little cozier on a blustery day."

"I wish it would snow," said Sonny. "It's not winter without snow. And I want to build a space snowman."

"Let's begin our meeting with good deeds," said Mrs. Peters, passing around a plate of ginger snaps.

"Why are these called snaps?" asked Lisa.

"Because they snap at you, like a turtle," said Roger, running after Lisa with a snapping cookie. "Snap, snap!" he went at her nose.

Mrs. Peters clapped her hands. "Good deeds," she repeated.

Hands waved. Good deeds were things you did to help someone. Good Scouts helped people whenever they could.

Rachel waved her hand right in front of Mrs. Peters.

"I went to see my grandpa in the nursing

home," she said, "and I played chess with him."

"Good for you, Rachel," said Mrs. Peters. "I'll bet your grandpa was glad to see you."

"He was," said Rachel. "I won the chess game."

"Ho, ho," said Roger. "I'll bet your grandpa can't see those chess men, that's why you won."

"My grandpa can too see!" said Rachel, standing up and stamping her foot.

Mrs. Peters put her hand up for silence and pointed to Kenny Baker, Patty Baker's twin brother.

"I helped wash windows," he said.

"But my mom had to do them over because they got smeary," said Patty.

"The thought counts," said Mrs. Peters. "That was a good deed."

"I gave our cat a bath," said Lisa. "But she didn't like it."

"I helped Mrs. Johnson cross the street," said Sonny.

"Why couldn't she cross the street by herself?" asked Rachel.

"She's old," said Sonny.

"She can run faster than you can, Stone. She doesn't need any help," said Roger. "I saw her playing tennis this summer at the park."

"Well, I guess she really didn't want help," admitted Sonny.

"Remember, boys and girls," said Mrs. Peters. "Helping people who do not want help is not .a good deed."

Sonny turned red again. This time it was not from the cold.

After a few more good deeds and some more hot chocolate, the Pee Wees were warm as toast.

"What badge are we going to earn next?" asked Kevin.

The Pee Wees jumped up and down waiting to hear. They loved badges. They loved to earn them and get them and wear them. And it was time for a new one.

"That is just what I am going to tell you about now," said Mrs. Peters.

CHAPTER 2

Make-Believe Snow

"My news," she said, "is a field trip! We need to take a little trip to get this new badge."

"Field trips are for school," said Roger. "Are we just going to the Dairy Queen, or to the science museum?"

Roger was right. Molly did not want to go to an ice cream stand in winter. What kind of badge could they get at the Dairy Queen?

Mrs. Peters laughed.

"We are not going to the Dairy Queen," she said, "or to a museum. This field trip is farther away. We have to leave early in the

morning, and we won't get back till night-time. We'll have to ride in my van."

The Pee Wees cheered. This was more like it. A real trip out of town! Away from home for a day. Molly did not know where they were going, but a trip anywhere with the Pee Wees in the van sounded like fun. New things to see. New people to meet.

"Where are we going?" shouted Tim.

"What badge will we get?" asked Kenny.

"We are going skiing," said their leader. "There is a ski resort not far away called the Little Alps. They have small slopes for children, and instructors to help them learn."

Troop 23 cheered. They waved paper napkins and stamped their feet.

Tracy raised her hand. "Mrs. Peters, I went skiing with my cousin last year. I took my own skis and, and we rode on the rope tow."

"So did I," bragged Roger. "I've got skis too."

"Fine," said Mrs. Peters. "Then it won't be new to you. On this trip we will all rent skis, because there won't be room in the van to carry them. I have permission from all of your parents. We won't be using the ski lift because we will be on the beginners' slope."

"That's called the bunny slope, Mrs. Peters," said Rachel. "It's for real little kids."

Rachel's curls bounced as she sat down. Rat's knees, thought Molly. Rachel could probably ski like the skiers on TV. And so would Tracy and Lisa and Roger.

Molly had never skied in her life. She would probably break all her bones running into a tree.

"I don't know how to ski, Mrs. Peters," shouted Tim.

"You do not have to know how to ski. We will stay on the bunny slope, and it is very small. If you fall, you will not hurt yourself. The bunny slope is not dangerous."

Sonny burst into tears. "I can't ski," he cried. "I don't want to go to the Alpos."

The Pee Wees giggled. "It's the Little Alps, dummy," said Roger. "Not dog food!" All the boys made growling noises.

Even while everyone laughed at Sonny, Molly felt like being kind to him. She knew how it was to be afraid of something. To be the only one who was left out. And to have other kids pick on you.

"I'll help you," she whispered to Sonny. "If I can stand up myself, that is."

"I don't want any help," scoffed Sonny. "I'm not going to any Alps."

Rat's knees, thought Molly. Sometimes Sonny was so hard to help.

"Besides, there's no snow yet," said Sonny. "How can we ski if there's no snow? We can't ski on grass!"

Rachel sighed. "They make snow at ski resorts," she said.

"They do not!" said Sonny. "No person can make snow."

"Rachel is right," said their leader. "Ski lodges haul snow in, or make their own with a snow machine."

"I know how that works," said Kevin. "It's just like a refrigerator."

Kevin went on to explain about condensation and cool air and warm air meeting.

"Kevin knows a lot," whispered Mary Beth to Molly.

No one had to tell Molly that. That was one reason she was going to marry him.

"So there is plenty of snow at the Little Alps," concluded Mrs. Peters. "Even if there is no snow here."

Sonny did not look happy about make-believe snow.

"When are we leaving?" asked Kenny.

Mrs. Peters held up a calendar.

"Next Sunday," she said. "I have all of your parents' permission. I have a list here

18

of what to bring, what kind of clothes to wear, and what time to meet. It will be a fun-filled day, and we will be back here around suppertime so you can get a good night's rest for school on Monday."

The Pee Wees groaned. They didn't want to think of going back to school after such a fun field trip. Molly and Kevin and Mary Beth groaned too, even though they liked school and never minded going back. Molly wished there was school all summer long.

"Now I realize that we cannot learn how to ski in just one day and with just one lesson," said Mrs. Peters. "But this will be a start. It will give you an idea of the basics. And if we all pay attention, we'll be able to ski down the bunny slope and earn our ski badge."

Mrs. Peters held up the badge. It was beautiful, thought Molly. The badge was blue. There was a little red skier on it. And

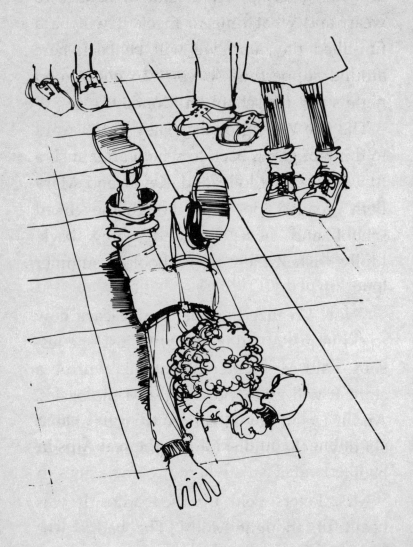

there was white snow falling behind him. Molly had to have it!

"I'll never get one!" cried Sonny, throwing himself onto the floor and wailing.

"Is there an advanced badge for those of us who know how to ski, Mrs. Peters?" asked Rachel.

"Yeah, I want a real ski badge," said Roger. "I don't want one for going down a bunny slope."

"We'll all get the same badge." Mrs. Peters frowned. "Pride goes before a fall, you know."

"What's that supposed to mean?" grumbled Roger.

"It means you might fall," said Tracy.

"Ha!" Roger laughed. "You won't catch me falling. I could ski down the real Alps in Switzerland. That's where my uncle goes to ski."

The Pee Wees talked about the field trip and the new badge they would earn. After that they told more good deeds, and then they got into a big circle in Mrs. Peters's kitchen and said the Pee Wee pledge and sang the Pee Wee song. What fun it was to be a Pee Wee Scout, thought Molly, squeezing Mary Beth's hand. And what fun it was to look forward to a field trip in the snow! She just hoped she could do what the instructor told her and ski down the bunny slope successfully.

She had to do well, because who else would help Sonny?

CHAPTER 3

Next Stop, the Little Alps

On the way home, all the Pee Wees could talk about was the field trip.

"I might wear my ski boots," said Rachel. "So I'll be ready to ski as soon as we get there."

"I'm wearing my new windbreaker," said Tracy.

"You need more than a windbreaker on those slopes," said Kenny.

When Molly got home, she got out her calendar. She put a big check mark on Sunday.

Every day she checked one day off the calendar. One day closer to the field trip.

Wednesday, checked off.

Thursday, checked off.

Friday, checked off.

On Saturday Molly's mother made checks too. Checks on the list of clothes and supplies to bring.

One warm jacket, checked off.

Snow pants, checked off.

Scarf, mittens, boots, sweater, checked off.

An apple and a snack bar, checked off.

A juice drink, checked off.

Finally it was Sunday morning. The weather was bright and sunny and not very cold.

"The weather forecast looks good," said Mr. Duff. "Warm and sunny and no rain or snow in sight! You'll have a good time on your trip!"

The Pee Wees came to Mrs. Peters's house all bundled up. Some of them could hardly walk! Sonny was the last one to arrive, and his mother was dragging him.

"I'm not going to those Alpos!" he cried.

"Sonny looks round and fat like a bear cub!" shouted Lisa.

"I'm hot," said Sonny, from under his scarf. "And I'm going home."

"I'm hot too," said Patty.

"We'll be glad to have warm clothes when we get on our skis," said their leader.

The Pee Wees piled in the Peterses' van. Mrs. Stone was going along too.

"I'm glad my mom isn't assistant Scout leader," said Mary Beth. "It wouldn't be any fun if your mother was along on a ski trip."

Molly agreed. "Sonny is used to being with his mother," she said. "But it isn't helping him be brave this time."

Mrs. Peters started the van. The Pee Wees cheered. Sonny screamed.

Mr. Peters stood in the front yard with baby Nick and waved.

Larry Stone, the fire chief, stood with the twins and waved too.

"Have fun!" the twins shouted.

"Don't get lost in a snowdrift on the bunny slope!" called Larry.

"That isn't the thing to say to Sonny." Molly frowned. "Doesn't Larry know he should say something encouraging?"

Adults did not understand children very well, thought Molly. Hadn't Mr. Stone ever been scared of anything when he was little?

The van started down the street. They were off on their adventure!

Molly and Mary Beth sat together. Sonny sat alone and pouted.

Mrs. Peters pulled onto the highway, and Mrs. Stone got out songbooks and led the Pee Wees in song. They sang the Pee Wee song and school songs and camping songs.

They sang "Row, Row, Row Your Boat" in a round.

After that Mrs. Stone gave them some skiing pointers. Like how to stop at the bottom of a hill. And how to walk up the hill with skis on, sideways.

"I know all that stuff," said Rachel.

"Then you can help show the others how it's done," said Mrs. Peters.

"You bet," said Rachel.

She liked to be a teacher, thought Molly. And she was good at it.

"Are we almost there?" asked Tim.

"Not yet," said Mrs. Peters. "But we will stop in the next town to have a little hot chocolate break and use the bathrooms."

The next town was called Round Lake. The Pee Wees scrambled into a restaurant called Nora's.

"I want a beefsteak," said Sonny, looking at the pictures on the menu. He appeared to have forgotten his fear of skis for the moment.

"This is just a hot chocolate break," Mrs. Peters reminded the Scouts.

But Sonny kept crying for beefsteak. Finally his mother sighed and ordered it for him. While the others drank their hot chocolate politely, Sonny tore away at a piece of steak, chewing loudly and rubbing his stomach to show how good it was.

"That is really bad manners," said Rachel. "To eat in front of all of us. And it's only ten o'clock in the morning! We just had breakfast."

"I think it's mean to eat a cow," said Patty. "They are so big and friendly and have such sad eyes. I think it's better to eat SpaghettiOs."

"Sonny's spoiled," said Tracy. "A spoiled baby."

After Sonny had eaten a few more bites, he left the rest of the beefsteak on his plate.

"It's too tough," he whined.

"Now we'll all go to the bathroom before we leave," said Mrs. Peters. She did not look happy with Sonny.

"I'll bet if his mother weren't here, Mrs. Peters would never buy Sonny a beefsteak dinner," said Kevin.

Molly and Mary Beth lined up at the door with the picture of a cowgirl on it. The boys lined up by the door with the cowboy on a bucking bronco.

All of a sudden Sonny got down from his chair and pushed ahead of the others. In his hurry he pushed open the cowgirl's bathroom instead of the cowboy's.

When he came out, his face was red.

The boys were laughing at him. "Hey, Stone, is your name Sally?" shouted Roger. "Are you a girl?"

"There are no words on the doors," said Sonny.

"They put pictures instead of words in case you can't read, dummy," said Roger.

31

The Pee Wees piled back into the van and played I Spy for the next ten miles.

"I spy something beginning with S," said Kenny.

"Scorpion," said Sonny.

"How could you see a scorpion out here?" asked Tracy. "Scorpions are in the desert."

"Is it animal, vegetable, or mineral?" asked Kevin.

Kenny thought a minute. "Animal," he said.

Now the Pee Wees were puzzled. They looked out the window and just saw the road and cornfields and sometimes a dog or cat or cow or horse. Nothing began with an S that they could see.

"Give up?" asked Kenny triumphantly.

They did.

"Scout leader!" said Kenny, pointing to Mrs. Peters.

The Pee Wees groaned.

"Look!" said Rachel, pointing out the window. "I see something beginning with *S!* Snow!"

Sure enough, there were snowflakes falling. But just a few.

The van went up a hill and down another. Then through a woods and over a little bridge. And then just when the Pee Wees could not think of another game to play in the car, they saw a sign: THE LITTLE ALPS SKI RESORT. There was a picture of a skier on one side and a small mountain on the other.

"Next stop," called Mrs. Peters, "the ski lodge!"

She drove the van in front of a big log building and said, "All out!"

The Pee Wees tumbled out of the van. All of them but Sonny.

"I'm staying right here," he said, holding on to the door of the van.

But between Mrs. Stone and Mrs. Peters, they pulled him out.

The lodge was on top of a big hill. From where they were, the Pee Wees could see smaller hills in all directions. People were little red and green and blue dots skiing down the hills. Other bright dots were riding the ski tow up the hills. Their skis dangled beneath them.

"I want to ride on that!" shouted Patty. She pointed to the ski lift.

The leaders laughed.

"On the hills we will ski," said Mrs. Peters, "we will just use a rope tow."

The leaders went inside and registered. They came out with tags to pin on all the Pee Wees' jackets.

"This shows that you are with the Pee Wee Scouts, and it will allow us to rent the skis," said Sonny's mother.

Troop 23 headed toward the slopes. Roger and Rachel raced ahead.

"I'm heading for that great big hill over there," said Roger, pointing.

Before long, the Pee Wees would be on skis, thought Molly. And she would find out if that little blue and white and red badge would be hers or not!

CHAPTER 4

Warming Up

"Let me introduce myself," said a tall man with shiny skis and a bright red jacket. He had a ski hat on and ski goggles, and in his mittened hands he had ski poles.

He came swooshing up in front of the Pee Wees, and his skis slid to a stop in a flash, sending a shower of white snow all over them.

"I'm Harry York, and I will be your ski instructor today. Call me Harry."

"I can't ski," cried Sonny to Harry.

"That's what I'm here for!" said Harry.

"How do you stop?" called Mary Beth.

"How do you start?" asked Kenny.

"How do you keep from falling?" shouted Tim.

Harry held up his hand. "One thing at a time." He laughed. "First we have to get you all some skis."

The Pee Wees followed him to a building. The building was full of skis!

Long ones and short ones.

Red ones and green ones and blue ones.

There were poles and boots and mittens and people trying them all on.

Harry slipped his own skis off and led them over to a big scale.

One by one he weighed and measured the Pee Wees.

"Hey, this is like going to the doctor!" shouted Sonny. "I'm not sick!"

"Do we get a lollipop?" asked Roger, stretching to make himself taller.

"This is so we can get the right size skis for you," said Harry.

Molly did not know that skis came in sizes.

Rachel was busy taking off her jacket and boots and ski pants.

"It wouldn't be my actual weight with all that stuff on," she said.

"We allow for that," said Harry. "You can leave all your wraps on."

"Rachel's afraid she's too fat!" Roger said, laughing.

"I am not," said Rachel crossly. "I just want to be accurate."

When the Pee Wees all had the right skis, Harry and the Scout leaders helped them buckle on the ski boots. Harry asked each Pee Wee if he or she had been on skis before.

"If you are used to skiing, we adjust the skis tighter," he said. "If you are brand new at skiing, we adjust them looser. That way when you fall, the skis will come off more easily."

"He said *when* you fall, not *if* you fall," Mary Beth pointed out to Molly. "He must think we aren't very good at it."

"Well, we aren't," said Molly.

"Fasten mine good and tight," said Rachel. "I'm a good skier. I have my own skis."

"Mine too," said Roger, not to be outdone by Rachel. "Tighter than hers."

"I'm not getting on those things," said Sonny. "No way."

When Molly saw a chance, she went up behind Sonny and whispered to him.

"You don't want to be the only one without a badge, do you? Lots of us haven't skied before, and we're trying it!"

Sonny glared at Molly. He looked as if he might give her a push out the door and into a drift.

"Come on! You can do it! It's a real little hill," Molly added.

Sonny looked out the door at the bunny slope. Molly thought he was going to cry all over again, but he said, "Well, all right."

It had worked! Molly had helped him! Maybe someday, with her help, Sonny would grow up!

Soon the Pee Wees were outside. Their skis were strapped on. They were lined up in a row. The bunny slope looked very steep to Molly.

"The first thing we do is warm up," said Harry.

Harry showed them how to do arm swings.

He showed them how to do ankle exercises.

He showed them how to lean sideways. Way to the right. Way to the left.

And he showed them how to fall without getting hurt.

The Pee Wees swung their arms. They leaned sideways. And they fell into the snow with their skis waving. Molly knew that before long they would have to actually go down the hill.

"The first thing we learn," said Harry, "is the snowplow."

As the Pee Wees watched, Harry stood with his skis almost meeting at the toes.

"We want to make an upside-down *V* with our skis," he said. "That is the best way to go down the hill."

Molly made her skis into an upside-down *V*.

Rachel did too.

But Sonny and Tim and Patty made their *V* go the wrong way.

Harry turned their skis the right way. "Toes together," he said. "But not crossing. If they cross, you'll take a tumble right off."

Soon all the Pee Wees were snowplows.

"Harry, where are our ski poles?" asked Rachel.

"We don't use poles here for beginners," he said. "Poles impede technique."

"What does that mean?" Mary Beth asked Molly.

Molly shook her head.

"That means it is easier to ski when you have more freedom," Harry said, as if he'd heard her. "You are free to put your arms out like wings, for balance."

All of the Pee Wees pretended they had wings.

"Is this stuff real snow?" asked Sonny.

"It's partly artificial snow and partly real snow," said Harry.

"Now the next rule to remember at all times," he went on, "is to bend the knees."

Harry leaned forward and put his hands on his knees.

"Never bend from the waist," he said. "Bend from the knees. And keep your eyes straight ahead on the bottom of the hill."

"There's too much to remember," cried Sonny. "I can't remember everything to do."

"Yes, you can," whispered Molly. "Just bend your knees and make an upside-down V with your skis."

"I want to get down that hill," said Rachel impatiently.

"Yeah, let's get going," said Roger. "This is boring."

Harry skied up behind each Pee Wee and made sure they made an upside-down V.

He made sure they were snowplows.

He made sure they bent their knees.

And he made sure there was plenty of space between each Pee Wee so they wouldn't run into each other.

Then he adjusted his goggles. "Let's go!" he said.

Off the Pee Wees went! Molly felt herself moving along slowly. She was skiing! She was really and truly skiing!

"Bend the knees," shouted Harry, as he skied in and out among the Scouts.

Rachel flew ahead of the others and was down at the bottom of the hill in a flash.

Molly wanted to look back and encourage Sonny. But when she did, she did not see Sonny. She saw Roger! Roger had tripped over his skis and was head over heels in a snowbank!

CHAPTER 5

Bend the Knees!

Tracy came alongside of Roger and veered into him! Behind Tracy came Lisa. Lisa bumped into Tracy. All three Scouts were tangled up, and skis were pointing in all directions.

"Darn these skis!" shouted Roger.

"He can't get them off"—Mary Beth laughed—"because he said he was a good skier and to make them tight!"

Molly and Mary Beth were halfway down the bunny slope, when all of a sudden someone shot by them.

"That was Sonny!" shouted Mary Beth. "Just look at him go!"

Sure enough, when Molly looked, Sonny was at the bottom of the hill beside Rachel!

"Boy, that was easy," said Sonny, when the others arrived. "You were right, Molly."

After all the fuss Sonny made, thought Molly, he turned out to be almost as good a skier as Rachel!

"Beginner's luck," said Rachel.

Sonny had grabbed on to the rope tow and was at the top of the hill again! Down he came once more, with his knees bent and his skis making a fine $\wedge$.

"He's good!" said Mary Beth. "And he wouldn't even be out here if you hadn't helped him!"

At the top of the hill, Harry and the two leaders were trying to pull Roger out of the snow. Tracy and Lisa got up and skied down. But as soon as Roger was on his feet, he tripped and fell again. "Try not to cross your skis," said Harry. "They should be close, but not touching."

"These are dumb skis," Roger grumbled.

Tim fell when he was halfway down the hill. And so did Patty and Kevin. But they got up and began again.

"This is fun!" called Sonny, whizzing by for the third time.

"You are a natural at it," said Harry.

The Pee Wees took the rope tow to the top and whizzed down again.

Over and over. Up and down. Down and up. Rachel and Sonny moved on to the next little hill. The only one who was not having fun was Roger.

"Pride goes before a fall," Mary Beth reminded him.

"Mind your own business," said Roger, brushing himself off.

"It looks like everyone made it down the hill but Roger," said Molly.

Now Molly began to feel sorry for Roger instead of Sonny. If he didn't get his ski badge, he would be very cross. And he would take it all out on the other Pee Wees.

"He has a terrible temper," said Mary Beth.

Roger was kicking snow at the others when they got near.

"I think we should help him," said Molly.

"He'd push us away," said Mary Beth.

"All he has to do to get his badge is go down the hill once," said Molly. "We could put him between us and hold him up all the way down. Mrs. Peters didn't actually say we had to go down by ourselves."

As the girls watched, Mrs. Peters gave Roger a tug. He stood up, started down the hill, and tumbled into a drift.

Harry pulled him up and showed him how to make a $\wedge$ and how to bend his knees. Roger did. But as soon as he started to move, the $\vee$ disappeared. Down he went.

"Let's go help him," said Molly, who was determined to see Roger get a badge.

The girls took hold of the rope and got pulled to the top. They skied up beside Roger.

"Get out of here," he said. "Leave me alone."

"Listen to us," said Molly, who would have stamped her foot if it hadn't had a ski on it. "Just hold on to us and you can make it. You can get down the hill and you can get your badge."

The girls grabbed his arm, one on each side.

"Bend your knees!" ordered Molly.

"Make a snowplow," said Mary Beth.

Roger was big. And he was heavy. It was not easy to hold him up.

But they were moving! Roger was not falling! They were skiing, all three of them. When they got to the bottom of the hill, Roger was still on his feet!

"Hurray!" cheered the Pee Wees, shouting and clapping.

Roger looked embarrassed. But he looked pleased too.

"That was fun," he said. Then under his breath so no one could hear, he muttered, "Thanks."

Just then Sonny swished up to Roger and said, "What a big baby! Had to have help from the girls." Then he skied off.

"Now Sonny ruined it all," said Molly in disgust.

"No, he didn't," said Rachel. "Roger deserves that. He's always calling Sonny a baby. It's about time the shoe is on the other foot."

"Or the ski." Tracy laughed.

The Pee Wees skied up and down the bunny slope together. By the end of the afternoon, Roger skied a few feet by himself. Real snow was falling gently, and the sun popped in and out behind the clouds. It was a beautiful day at the Little Alps.

"How many are ready for some cocoa at the lodge?" asked Mrs. Peters.

Mittens waved. They all clamored up the slope on the rope tow together. Harry helped them check in their skis and put their own boots back on.

"It feels funny to walk!" shouted Sonny.

"It feels like it does after you skate!" said Mary Beth.

The Pee Wees all trooped back to the lodge. There was a big fire in the fireplace. They sat around it and sang their Pee Wee song while their leaders brought cocoa and apples and some cheese to snack on.

Molly was warm and sleepy and full of good feelings after such a fun day with her friends. And they still had the long cozy ride home in the van.

No one noticed that the fluffy light snowflakes had turned into heavy wet ones, or that a strong gust of wind had come up from the north.

CHAPTER 6

Stuck in a Drift

As the Pee Wees piled into the van, they noticed the sun had gone down and that even though it was afternoon, it was getting dark.

The van had gone along merrily for several miles when Mrs. Peters said, "There is a wind coming up."

Molly noticed the trees waving and bending. Their leaders were frowning. They had worried looks on their faces.

No one felt like playing I Spy. No one felt like singing. They all just sat and looked out the window at the snow. Every minute it seemed to get heavier. Soon they could not

see the farmhouses along the road, or the cornfields. In a little while they could not even see the road! Mrs. Peters had the headlights on, and the windshield wipers and the defroster, and she looked nervous.

"It's very slippery," she said to Mrs. Stone. "We have to go very, very slowly."

"Look!" called Lisa. "There's a car in the ditch."

Sure enough, right beside them on the edge of the road was a car that could not move.

Pretty soon they saw lots of cars that could not move, but no one said anything about them. But they were all thinking the same thing, thought Molly. They were all thinking they might be the next one in the ditch!

"I read in the paper some hunters got lost in a snowstorm," said Rachel. Her voice sounded shaky. "They froze."

"Now don't worry about a thing," said

Mrs. Peters, a little too brightly. "We are not lost."

Not yet, thought Molly. But what if they got lost? What if they froze like the hunters?

"Let's just relax and sing a song," said Mrs. Peters in a fake cheery voice. "Or maybe it would be a good idea to take a little nap."

But no one could sing. And no one could sleep.

"The gas thing is almost on empty!" cried Tracy.

"We have plenty of gas," said Mrs. Peters. "We'll be just fine."

But Molly knew things were not fine. She wondered how long they could live in the van with no gas and no food or water. And no bathroom!

"I think we should try to stop in the next town," said Mrs. Peters. "I can't see to drive."

At the next road, their leader turned off

the highway, and with a shudder and a leap forward, the van landed in a big drift. Mrs. Peters tried to open the van door, but it would not open.

She pushed. She shoved. Mrs. Stone pushed and shoved. But the drift was so high that the door would not budge.

"I'm afraid this is as far as we can go," said Mrs. Peters.

No one knew what to say. "The main thing is we must not panic," said their leader. "It is best to sit right here and keep warm and wait for help to arrive."

"What help, Mrs. Peters?" moaned Tracy. "We're all alone out here."

"It just feels that way," said Mrs. Stone. "There are people not far from here. We just can't see them in a storm."

Molly wasn't sure that was true. The only people around for miles were ones that were stuck in drifts just as they were. They were in the country. And the country could go on for miles with just trees and telephone poles and cornfields.

"I'm hungry!" cried Sonny.

"We have a little food," said Mrs. Peters. "But we have to save it. We have a little fruit and some crackers and a little grapefruit juice."

"I'm allergic to grapefruit, Mrs. Peters," said Rachel.

Mrs. Peters was trying to be cheerful, but Molly could see that her patience was limited.

"Then you will just have to drink melted snow," she replied.

"There are germs in snow!" shouted Tim. "And maybe even acid rain."

Mrs. Peters sighed. "Boys and girls," she said, "this is an emergency. We don't have any choice about what we eat or drink. We are lucky to have any food at all. Do you understand?"

The Pee Wees nodded. This was no picnic.

This was no ski trip anymore. This was an emergency, like the emergencies on TV.

"I think we should call 911," said Sonny. "That's what you're supposed to do in an emergency."

Now even Mrs. Stone sighed. "No 911 people could get here, Sonny, even if we did have a phone. They couldn't get their rescue vehicles out in this storm. We all have to pull together and be very brave. We must act maturely and responsibly and work for the good of the group. There is no room for babies."

"Ha," whispered Mary Beth. "Her own kid is the only baby here."

The Pee Wees huddled together in the van. The snow blew against the windows, and the wind whistled through the trees.

"My feet are frozen," said Rachel.

"So are mine," said Mary Beth. "I can't feel my toes!"

"Let's jiggle our feet," said Mrs. Stone.

"Up and down, up and down, till they warm up."

The Pee Wees jiggled. Up and down and sideways.

"Pretend we are running, while we are sitting in one place," said Mrs. Stone. "That is what joggers do to warm up."

The Pee Wees ran in place. Then they jiggled some more. Mrs. Stone was right, thought Molly. She did feel warmer. Pretty soon they were all laughing. And laughing warmed them all up.

Suddenly Tim's hand went up. "Mrs. Peters, my mother is expecting me home tonight. She'll be really mad if I don't come home."

Sonny burst into tears again. "I don't want to stay here overnight!" he cried. "I'm homesick. I want to go home right now."

"Then you'll have to walk," said Kevin.

"How can he be homesick when his mother is right here?" whispered Mary Beth in Molly's ear. "He's the only one who shouldn't be homesick!"

Molly felt homesick too. Homesick and scared. She did not want to be brave. What would happen if it kept snowing?

If no one came and rescued them?

What if they had to live in this van forever? Would she have to live with Sonny and Roger? Would she grow up and get old and have only the clothes on her back? She might never see her parents again!

And what would happen when the food was gone?

As if she could hear Molly's thoughts, Rachel said, "I saw a thing on a news show where these people up on a mountain were trapped by a blizzard and didn't have any food at all after three days. Do you know what they did?"

"Fell asleep," said Tim.

"Ate trees," said Kenny.

"Died," said Lisa.

Rachel shook her head. "They ate each other," she said.

Now the Pee Wees were really alarmed. No one wanted to eat each other! This was no emergency. This was a crisis. This was the stuff TV movies were made of.

"Well, I'm not eating Roger!" said Mary Beth.

"He'd be tough to chew," said Rachel.

Mrs. Peters put her hand up. "No one will eat each other," she said firmly. "We will be out of here very soon."

"Mrs. Peters, I could shovel us out of here. There's a shovel in the back here," said Kevin.

"Thank you very much, Kevin, but it would be dangerous to get out of the van even if we could open the doors. No one could see you in the snow, and you could wander off and get lost. I think it is wisest to sit tight and wait for help. The snowplows will have to come by, and then the police will be able to rescue people."

Their leader's words sounded very sensible. But when would all this happen? thought Molly. Before or after they froze to death?

CHAPTER 7

Rescued!

"**W**e should send smoke signals to get help," said Kenny. "We have matches in the emergency kit."

"We can't make a fire in the wet snow," scoffed Roger.

"But Kenny does have a good idea," said their leader. "We should do something to attract attention so that if searchers come by, they won't miss us."

"I have a bright red scarf, Mrs. Peters," said Rachel. "You could use it as a flag."

"That's a wonderful idea," said Mrs. Peters. "We'll roll down the window and fasten it onto the antenna."

Kevin scrambled into the front seat. He opened the window and crawled partway out. He grabbed the wire and tied Rachel's scarf to it.

"Now someone will see us," he said.

But more time went by, and no one did. The Pee Wees jiggled their feet and ate the snacks and wrapped themselves up in blankets from the back of the van.

They did some crossword puzzles from Mrs. Peters's emergency kit and tried to take a little nap.

Just as Molly was dozing off and dreaming that a spaceship had come down to rescue them, she heard a loud scraping noise.

"It's a snowplow!" yelled Roger. He opened one of the windows and waved his mittens at it.

"The snow has stopped falling!" said Mrs. Stone.

The snowplow man waved as he sped by

74

and shouted some words that were lost on the wind.

"It won't be long now," said Mrs. Peters.

As soon as the plow went by, some of the cars began to follow it very slowly. But the van was in the drift too deep to get back on the road.

Suddenly flashing red lights lit up the sky. A siren sounded, and a police van with big snow tires pulled up beside the drift the van was in.

Sonny rolled a window down and flung himself through it into the arms of a policeman. "Save us!" he shrieked.

The two policemen got the van doors open, checked to see that no one was hurt, and said, "The tow trucks are on their way. Meanwhile, you get in our van, and we'll take you in to warm up."

"Are you taking us to jail?" asked Patty in alarm.

The policeman laughed. "It's no crime to be stuck in a drift, young lady," he said. "We'll just get you warmed up and find a place for you to stay for the night."

"The night?" shrieked the Pee Wees.

"I'm afraid it will be too late to drive by the time the van is towed," he said. "In the morning the roads will be safer."

The leaders thanked the policemen. "If it weren't for you, we'd be in that drift all night!"

"It was a good idea to put the scarf out," said the policeman. "It was easier to spot you."

At the police station the Pee Wees had more hot chocolate. Then a lady named Mrs. Sparrow said the Pee Wees were welcome to sleep on her floor on blankets. The police officers knew her, and she had a big house. She made them hot dogs for supper, and Mrs. Peters called home to tell the parents not to worry.

"A slumber party!" said Tracy.

In the morning Mrs. Sparrow made the Pee Wees ham and eggs, and then they got into the snowy van that the tow truck pulled to her driveway.

"Thank you!" called the Pee Wees, waving.

On the way home, Mrs. Peters said, "You were all very very brave. You were exactly what Scouts should be."

"I wasn't scared at all," said Sonny. "It was fun."

Molly wanted to blurt out that Sonny had been a big scared baby most of the time!

"It was a piece of cake," said Roger. "I wish we could have been out there longer."

"Sure, White, you can say that now," said Rachel.

"Do you know what?" said Lisa. "We get off school today! Everyone else is in school today."

Now a new cheer went up in the van.

"No school! No school! No school!" chanted the Pee Wees.

"Don't drive too fast, Mrs. Peters," said Kenny. "We don't want to get home too early."

Just a little while ago the Pee Wees had been worried they wouldn't ever get home at all, thought Molly. And now here they were trying to delay it.

But even with the snowy roads, the trip home seemed to go faster than when they came. The trucks had plowed, and now they were sanding the road so that cars would not slip on the ice.

When the van drew up in front of the Peterses' house, parents seemed to burst out of the doors to meet them!

"We were so worried!" cried Mr. and Mrs. Duff.

"Imagine, gone overnight in a snow-storm!" said Tracy's father.

"The TV station called and wants to inter-view the Pee Wees," said Mr. Peters.

So after the Pee Wees and their leaders had rested awhile, they trooped to the TV studio to be interviewed.

"Can you tell us in your own words how it felt to be out in one of the greatest storms of the decade?" said a bald man with a mi-crophone. "How did it feel to be in danger, and without food?"

"I wasn't scared," said Sonny. "There's no room for babies in an emergency. You have to act really grown up and brave."

"Sonny is lying," whispered Mary Beth. "That is an outright lie."

"Maybe he has his fingers crossed," said Molly. "And he was a little bit brave for that one hour."

"How did you feel?" asked the bald man, putting the microphone in front of Molly.

"I was really scared," said Molly. "I was afraid we would freeze in a big drift."

"I was afraid we'd have to eat each other," said Tim.

"We are grateful to be alive and well and home again," said Mrs. Peters at the end of the interview. "The Pee Wees were good Scouts in the emergency."

The Pee Wees filed out after the show and ran to Mrs. Peters's house to watch themselves on TV. Some of the parents were there too. After the news, the Pee Wees told everyone about their ski trip.

"It seems like weeks ago," said Molly. "And it was only yesterday."

"Now," said Mrs. Peters, clapping her hands, "I have something for all of us. It seems like a good time to give out our new badges while we all are together."

Mrs. Peters called each Scout's name and handed out the blue and white and red ski badges. Everyone clapped extra loud when Roger's name was called, and no one teased him.

On the way home, Molly told her parents what a good time she had skiing.

She told them about helping Sonny be brave and helping Roger get down the hill.

"You worked hard the last two days," said Mr. Duff. "I think you need a good rest tonight."

Molly yawned. "I know one thing," she said. "I don't want to go anywhere in a car in winter again for a long, long time."

"By tomorrow, you'll be ready to go again," her father teased.

Maybe he was right. If it was another trip with the Pee Wee Scouts, Molly wouldn't want to miss it.

Pee Wee Scout Song
(to the tune of
"Old MacDonald Had a Farm")

Scouts are helpers, Scouts have fun,
Pee Wee, Pee Wee Scouts!
We sing and play when work is done,
Pee Wee, Pee Wee Scouts!

With a good deed here,
And an errand there,
Here a hand, there a hand,
Everywhere a good hand.

Scouts are helpers, Scouts have fun,
Pee Wee, Pee Wee Scouts!

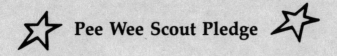

Pee Wee Scout Pledge

We love our country
And our home,
Our school and neighbors too.

As Pee Wee Scouts
We pledge our best
In everything we do.